This book belongs to:

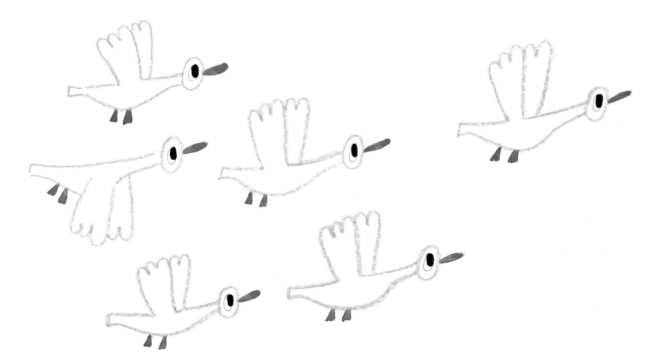

Quarto is the authority on a wide range of topics.

Quarto educates, entertains and enriches the lives of
our readers—enthusiasts and lovers of hands-on living.

www.quartoknows.com

Author and Illustrator: Dubravka Kolanovic
Designer: Victoria Kimonidou
Editor: Harriet Stone

© 2018 Quarto Publishing plc

First Published in 2018 by QED Publishing,
an imprint of The Quarto Group.
The Old Brewery, 6 Blundell Street,
London N7 9BH, United Kingdom.
T (0)20 7700 6700 F (0)20 7700 8066
www.QuartoKnows.com

A catalogue record for this book is available from
the British Library.

ISBN 978 1 91241 391 1

Manufactured in Guangdong, China CC072018

9 8 7 6 5 4 3 2 1

FSC
www.fsc.org

MIX
Paper from
responsible sources
FSC® C008047

True Friends

by DUBRAVKA KOLANOVIC

Fox was raking fallen leaves in his
garden when he heard someone crying.

"Oh dear! Whoever can
that be?" Fox wondered.

Fox followed the sobs until, behind
a tree, he found a goose in tears.

"What's the matter, Goose?" asked Fox.

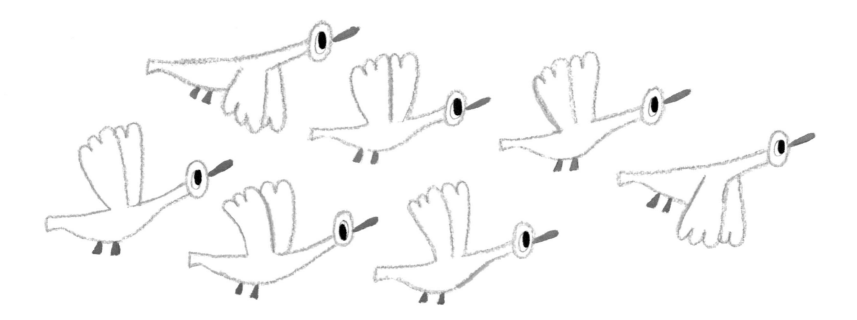

"My flock has left me behind!" she cried,
pointing at the sky. "And I don't
know where they are going."

Fox felt very sorry for the goose. Then he had an idea.

"Jump into my wheelbarrow. I will help you
catch up with your friends," he said.

Goose climbed into the wheelbarrow, but no matter how fast Fox ran, he couldn't catch up with the geese.

"I have a better idea," Fox said.

Fox and Goose boarded a train.
The train went really fast.

Uphill and downhill it
sped, until Fox and Goose
saw the flock above them.

They were heading towards a big city.

The city was so big and so busy, Goose thought she had lost her flock again. But Fox had another idea. He and Goose climbed a very tall skyscraper.

Looking across the city, they
were able to spot Goose's flock
flying towards the ocean.

They raced to the port.
"Let's rent a boat," said Fox.
Goose was glad Fox was
with her. He always had
such good ideas.

The pair watched the geese from their boat. "I think they're flying to a warmer place for the winter," said Fox.

Clever Fox was right!
After several days at sea the
geese flew down to an island.
Goose and Fox carefully
landed their boat.

Goose was excited to be reunited with her flock. "Thank goodness, Goose, you made it!" they cried. She ran towards them with her wings open wide.

Soon it was time for Fox to leave.
Goose hugged Fox goodbye and
thanked him for all his help.

Fox boarded the boat and got ready
to set sail. He felt sad and wondered
if he'd ever see his friend again.

Suddenly there came a voice from the island. "True friends should stick together! Will you stay with us, Fox?"

The geese were very
grateful to Fox and wanted
him to stay. He was a true
friend because he had been
there for Goose when she
needed him most.

Fox was so pleased!
He stayed on the island
with Goose and her flock
all winter, playing games
and telling stories.

Uphill and down, over the city
and across the sea, Fox and Goose were
true friends. Now and always.

Next Steps

Discussion and comprehension

Discuss the story with the children and ask the following questions, encouraging them to take turns and give full answers if they are able to. Offer support by turning to the appropriate pages of the book for support if needed.

- Who are the characters in this story?
- Why did Fox feel sorry for Goose at the start of the story?
- What kinds of transport did Fox and Goose use on their journey?
- Why do you think some buildings are called skyscrapers?
- Why do you think that birds go to warmer places in the winter?
- Who is your truest friend? Why?

Postcard Home

At the end of the story, the geese ask Fox to stay with them, as he has been such a good friend. Ask the children why they think Fox wanted to stay. Ask the children if they think anyone will be wondering where Fox is. Show examples of postcards and explain that when people go to places far away they can send postcards home, so that their friends and family can see where they are and what they are doing. Give the children a template of a postcard where they can draw a picture of the island on one side and write a message home on the other. Model an example first, showing the children to write about where Fox is, what he is doing, who he is with and when he will be home.

Fox or Goose Bookmark

Cut rectangular pieces of orange or white card and round the edges. Fold each card in half lengthways and draw a diagonal line, starting at the crease ¼ of the way up and finishing in the middle of the folded half, about ¾ of the way up. Give each child one of the cards and ask them to cut along this line. When they have made this cut and opened out the card, they will have one piece with a V-shape in the middle, which will hold the page of a book. This 'V' can form Fox's snout or Goose's beak. The children can use felt tips or crayons to colour the beak or snout and draw on any details.

When Fox meets a goose who has been
left behind by her flock, he decides to help
her catch up with her migrating friends.

Fox and Goose go on an epic journey, through
the city and across the sea, learning along
the way what being a true friend really means.

Beautifully illustrated, **QED Storytime**
introduces young children to the pleasures of
reading and sharing stories. Next Steps provide
guidance for parents and teachers.

£5.99

ISBN 978-1-91241-391-1